Maud Lewis: Artist

Heather Rising

Contents

Maud Lewis: Artist

Who Was Maud Lewis?

Maud Lewis was a famous Canadian painter. She was known for making a kind of colourful art called **folk art**.

This is Maud Lewis in 1965, when she was around 64 years old.

Maud was born in 1901. She grew up in a small town in a part of Canada called Nova Scotia (say: *No-va Sko-sha*), and began painting as a child.

Painting was never easy for Maud. She was born with a disease called **arthritis**, which caused her spine and fingers to be bent. But Maud found joy in painting and she continued to paint her whole life.

Maud sold her paintings of colourful country **scenes** from her house. She became well known across Canada and, later, around the world.

Maud liked to paint the countryside around her home.

Maud's Early Life

Maud had a happy childhood with her parents, John and Agnes, and her brother, Charles. Her father was a **blacksmith** and the family had enough money to live comfortably.

Maud could do all the things other children did, despite her disabilities. In the early 1900s, girls did not always go to school. But Maud went to school. The other children were not always kind to her because she looked different. Maud left school early at only 14 years old.

As a child, Maud had a cat called Fluffy.

Maud learnt to play the piano. She kept playing until she had to stop because the arthritis in her hands made it too painful.

Maud was taught to paint by her mother. They used **watercolour paints** to make Christmas cards, and together they sold them in the neighbourhood for five cents each.

Maud kept painting Christmas cards, like this one, as an adult.

Maud's Adult Life

Maud lived in her childhood home until her parents died when she was in her 30s. Her brother sold the house. Maud did not **inherit** anything.

In 1938, Maud moved in with an aunt for a short time. She soon found a job in a town about 100 kilometres away. A man named Everett Lewis **hired** Maud as his housekeeper. Maud moved in with Everett and, soon after, they were married. Maud was 37 years old.

Maud and Everett lived in a tiny house in Nova Scotia.

Maud and Everett did not have very much money.
They lived in a tiny, one-room house.
The house had no running water or electricity.

Maud and Everett's house only had one room.

Everett sold fish door-to-door in their town. Maud went with him and sold greeting cards that she painted.

Over the years, Maud's arthritis got worse.
Her hands and fingers became twisted.
Even though the house was very small,
Maud was not able to do the chores.

Soon, Maud could no longer go with Everett
to sell her cards for extra money.
Instead, she sat at home by their small window
and painted in the natural light.

Maud painted by a small window in her house.

Everett found pieces of board for Maud and she began to paint scenes on them.

Maud sold these works of art from her home. She painted a sign that said "PAINTINGS FOR SALE" and put it where people could see it as they passed by on the road.

This is Maud holding one of her paintings outside her home.

Maud's Art

Materials

Maud did not always buy the paint she painted with. Everett sometimes brought home leftover cans of paint for her. The paint had been used on fishing boats and houses around Nova Scotia, so the colours were often very bright.

Nova Scotia is known for its brightly coloured boats and buildings.

When Maud had some money, she would buy tubes of **oil paints**. Most of her paintings were quite small, only about the size of a magazine. She sold her paintings for two or three dollars each, sometimes a little more.

Maud also painted for herself.
With only a **wood stove** for heat and lanterns for light,
Maud filled the house with images.
She painted all the cupboards, walls and even the windows
with flowers and animals.
Maud's colourful artwork brightened the house during
the long, dark winters.

The inside of Maud's home was a cheerful place.

What Maud Painted

Because Maud did not travel often, she painted hundreds of pictures of things she remembered from her childhood.

Maud painted the leaves turning brilliant orange and red in the autumn.

Maud loved showing the colours of autumn in her artwork.

Many of her pictures show people enjoying the winter while sledding down hills. Others show horses pulling sleighs through fresh snow.

In Maud's bright spring paintings, green hills slope down to the coast. She filled blue oceans with fishing boats and the sky with puffy clouds and seagulls.

Coastal villages filled Maud's springtime paintings.

Maud also painted houses sitting in summer fields filled with colourful blooms. She often painted cats sitting in flowers.

Maud's paintings showed the best parts of each season in Nova Scotia.

One of Maud's more well-known paintings is of a cat and her two kittens.

How Maud Painted

Maud worked on a painting without stopping, until it was finished. She used short, quick brush strokes to fill in her paint. Maud's paintings were often small because of the size of the boards she had.

Many artists blend their own paint colours, but Maud didn't often mix her paints. She used them exactly as they were when Everett brought them home. It meant that her colours were bold and strong. They reminded people of the houses and boats in the local area.

Maud's art showed the lives of the people who lived and worked near her.

Maud liked painting the scenes she saw around her, like this horse working in the snow.

This painting shows a cheerful scene of people driving through the town in their car.

Maud painted people enjoying themselves in nature and while they worked. She did not paint dark, stormy skies or shadowy forests. Her works were bright and cheerful.

A Successful Artist

Maud's colourful house attracted visitors who came to look at her art. Her hopeful pictures of spring blooms, green farm fields and sunny skies were charming. Visitors wanted to take those memories home with them.

After a while, Maud began to become well known. Travellers came to buy her art. People asked her to make paintings for them. She painted a set of window shutters someone had ordered for their cottage. Her paintings never sold for more than ten dollars.

Maud painted this lamp for someone's home.

Window shutters, like this one, were a popular item with Maud's customers.

In 1965, Maud became famous. A newspaper published a story about her and some photographs of her art. Soon after, a short film about her life was shown on a Canadian television program. More stories followed and more customers came to visit her home.

But Maud's arthritis had become very painful. She often had to visit the hospital. She had difficulty finishing the paintings that people had ordered.

Sadly, Maud died in 1970.

To celebrate Maud's life, a copy of her house was built in her hometown.

Maud's Gift

Since Maud's death, her life and art have become even more famous. There have been plays, books and films made about her life.

In 2019, the Canadian postal service put out a special stamp of Maud's painting *White Cat*. Maud's art is collected and displayed in art galleries across Canada.

The Art Gallery of Nova Scotia has had a special display of Maud Lewis's art since 1998.

Now, Maud's paintings sell for large sums of money. In 2017, one of her works sold for $40 000.

In 1984, when Maud's house began to crumble, it was moved to the Art Gallery of Nova Scotia. The house was **restored** and all the art inside it was saved. Now everyone can visit the house, and enjoy the happiness that painting brought to Maud Lewis.

Maud Lewis's house now sits inside the Art Gallery of Nova Scotia.

Why I Like Maud Lewis's Paintings

I was lucky enough to visit an art gallery in Nova Scotia in Canada, and learn about the folk artist Maud Lewis.

I was sorry to learn that Maud had problems with her hands. I know how bad it feels to be teased. But when I looked at Maud's paintings in the gallery, I didn't see any sadness.

I liked the paintings with animals the best. I felt very still when I saw a picture of a mother deer and her **fawn** standing together. The painting with the black cat and two kittens reminded me of how excited my cat gets when she spends time outside in the spring flowers.

This painting of a deer and her fawn made me feel so peaceful.

Maud's house is in the gallery, too. The house is so tiny – I don't know how two people could have lived there. I thought it would be dark inside because there weren't many windows. Then I looked through the door and I was surprised to see how bright it was. There were colourful birds and large flowers all over the cupboards, walls and windows. Butterflies were painted everywhere. It looked just like summertime inside. It made me smile.

I felt good after I saw where Maud lived. I think she would have been happy sitting by the window painting her pictures.

I enjoyed seeing the spot where Maud painted.

Maud must have loved to paint. All her pictures are bright and full of colour. I would buy one of Maud's paintings, if I could. I would hang it in my room and whenever I felt sad, I would look at it. It would make me think of summer and fun things to do. Soon, I would feel happy again.

I would love to own this painting of a horse in a field – it makes me happy.

Glossary

arthritis (*noun*)	a disease that causes painful swelling and stiffness at the point between two bones
blacksmith (*noun*)	a person who heats and shapes metal into tools or objects
fawn (*noun*)	a baby deer
folk art (*noun*)	artworks with bright, bold colours and designs, usually made by an untrained artist
hired (*verb*)	agreed to pay someone money to do a job
inherit (*verb*)	to receive money or property from someone after they die
oil paints (*noun*)	special paints that are thick and slow to dry
restored (*verb*)	fixed to how it was when first made
scenes (*noun*)	pictures of a place or setting

watercolour paints (*noun*)
special paints that are mixed with water

wood stove (*noun*) a stove that makes heat by burning wood

Index